FLASH

MISSIONS

SUPERSONIC

Go to www.maxflash.co.uk,
and enter this code:
JH30PS11LB29
for your freebies, downloads
and other Max Flash goodies

For Talia and Joe
Massive thanks to Lauren, Jane and
all the fantastic team at Stripes

STRIPES PUBLISHING
An imprint of Little Tiger Press
1 The Coda Centre, 189 Munster Road, London SW6 6AW

A paperback original
First published in Great Britain in 2007

ISBN: 978-1-84715-026-4

A CIP catalogue record for this book is available from the British Library.

Printed in China

2 4 6 8 10 9 7 5 3

MISSION 2

SUPERSONIC

Jonny Zucker

Illustrated by
Ned Woodman

CHAPTER 1

The sword came crashing down towards Max Flash, who thrust out his cutlass and managed to block the powerful blow.

But it only held off the Ninja Baboon for a few seconds.

Immediately, the creature smashed the sword towards Max's knees. Max leaped into the air and the weapon swished just millimetres below his body.

The Baboon shrieked with frustration and threw its sword on to the craggy ground.

It beat its chest in fury. Orange wisps of smoke poured out of its nostrils and shoots of stinking grey spittle flew out of its mouth.

Max tightened his grip on the cutlass and quickly scanned the darkened graveyard.

What should my next move be?

The Baboon breathed heavily, raising its giant fists and beginning to advance towards Max.

And then Max saw it – the Orb of Justice.

It was resting on top of a street lamp just beyond the graveyard wall, glowing with a flickering pulse of green light.

If I can outrun this monster, maybe I can make it to the Orb. The Ninja Baboon will be no match for the Orb's incredible powers.

Max suddenly remembered the smoke grenade in his pocket. In an instant he pulled it out and hurled it across the ground towards his enemy. The Baboon howled in terror and began to back off. Max started to run towards

the Orb. He didn't look back until he was halfway across the graveyard, and when he did he immediately wished he hadn't.

The Baboon's initial fear of the grenade had disappeared and the monkey was now thundering after Max, only a few metres behind him. Max upped his pace frantically. When he was five metres from the Orb he leaped into the air and reached out to grab the prize. Just as he made contact with it, he felt the Ninja Baboon's claw on his left ankle – and then he froze in mid-flight.

A second later, all signs of the Baboon, the Orb and the graveyard completely vanished. Max spun round. He was back in the living room and his mum was striding towards him with a serious expression on her face.

"Mum!" he protested loudly. "If I'd got the Orb I'd have made it to Level 7!"

"You can play computer games again later. Zavonne wants to see you," she informed him.

MAX FLASH

Max arched his left eyebrow and put his electronic control cutlass down on the table. *Zavonne? Is it time for my second mission?*

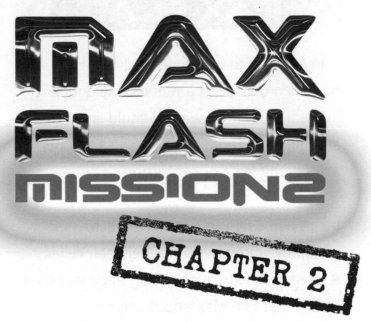

CHAPTER 2

Max had been introduced to Zavonne only very recently. It was his parents who'd taken him to her. And without a shadow of doubt, meeting Zavonne had been the biggest shock of his life.

Max's mum and dad were a stage magic double act. Max had grown up backstage in theatres and arts centres, watching his parents and a whole range of other magical acts. He studied their tricks, worked out how they were done and then perfected them himself.

In addition to his stage magic abilities, Max had been born with a remarkable double-jointedness that meant he could squeeze in and out of incredibly tight spaces and perform astounding feats of contortion.

Just over a month ago his parents had taken him down to a secret hi-tech communications centre under their cellar. A woman called Zavonne had appeared on a screen and told Max about the organisation she worked for – the DFEA; the Department for Extraordinary Activity.

She'd explained that the DFEA dealt with 'unusual' activities, things that would freak out the normal forces of law and order – like time travel and creatures from outer space. After revealing to Max that his parents had carried out two DFEA operations in the past, she then told him his own contortionist powers and skills with magic tricks and illusions made him a perfect choice to be a DFEA Operative.

Zavonne had enlisted Max's help in fighting
a computer game character called Deezil – a
terrifying lizard man who had been determined
to break free from the Virtual world and
imprison his creators, the human race. To
Max's astonishment, he had been transported
into the hard drive of a top programmer's
computer where he'd taken on crazed
speedway drivers, bloodthirsty centurions and
gruesome slime beasts (not to mention an
infuriating farm girl named Daisy Do-Good) on
his path to stopping Deezil's evil plan. It had
been a totally mad, terrifying and brilliant
adventure, and Max grinned at the thought of
a second mission.

Max's dad was waiting for Max and his mum
at the top of the steps leading down to the
cellar, and the three of them descended into
the dim light. Just like before, Max's dad
flicked a switch that moved a workbench over
against a wall, revealing a small panel in the

floor. He slid the panel aside and stood back.

Max looked at his parents' concerned faces. They'd come down with him to the Communications Centre the first time, but now he was a fully fledged DFEA Operative just him and Zavonne were to meet for his briefings and debriefings.

"Good luck," said Max's mum.

His dad squeezed Max's shoulder and gave him an encouraging smile.

Max lowered himself on to the ladder, and after his feet hit the floor at the bottom he flicked on the lights.

The Communications Centre was a square whitewashed room, the walls of which were dotted with high–tech silver equipment, black encased digital display panels and racks of red levers and green buttons.

On the wall facing Max was a giant, wafer-thin plasma screen.

It suddenly came to life and Zavonne's face

appeared, as ice-cool and unsmiling as the last time he'd seen her.

"We have a situation," said Zavonne briskly.

Great to see you too! Max thought sarcastically.

"It's connected to outer space," she continued. "Get ready for blast off, Max."

CHAPTER 3

Max eyed Zavonne incredulously.

Outer space?

Zavonne stared back without emotion.

"Forty years ago," she began, "a UFO crash-landed into a remote quarry, deep in the countryside."

Max had read loads of stuff about UFOs and had never seen anything that offered even the tiniest shred of hard evidence that such things existed. Mind you, he'd always assumed it was impossible to be sucked into

a computer's hard drive until he'd done it himself.

"The equipment used by the official authorities to monitor the skies was far too unsophisticated to pick up this craft," Zavonne continued, "but the DFEA spotted it. We rushed a team out there to see if it was a manned or unmanned flight. On board was a group of aliens. We instantly saw they meant us no harm. They were, in fact, in a very bad way: incredibly weak. Of course, the first problem was understanding what they were trying to tell us. It took us over a week to produce equipment that was complex enough to communicate properly with them. However, once we had the Speech Pulse Translator up and running, DFEA Operatives could finally understand what these aliens were saying and vice versa. The first thing they told us was that they were from the planet Zockra."

"Never heard of it," said Max.

"That's because Zockra exists in a galaxy beyond our solar system. The Hedra galaxy can only be entered through a tiny swirling vortex. No conventional astronaut or space scientist knows anything about it. There are many planets up there and the vast majority are inhabited by small groups of aliens."

"Why were the Zockrans so ill?" asked Max.

"As humans began to produce massive amounts of pollution, the chemicals and gases started to rise up through the hole in our ozone layer and slip through the vortex into their galaxy. While other alien peoples were not affected by these pollutants, the Zockrans started getting poisoned. Their mission to Earth was a last-ditch cry for help. They journeyed to the source of the pollution, exposing themselves to a massively strong dose of poison, to try and find an antidote. The DFEA took them in and looked after them in a top-secret laboratory, trying to work out how to save them."

Max was stunned.

"And did you?" he asked.

"After a huge programme of research and experiments, we eventually discovered that humans possess something called 'Aura Energy'. This energy slows down the poisoning process from the pollution we create. Without this energy, we'd all be dead by now. No one outside of the DFEA knows this energy exists."

"So the Zockrans needed some of this Aura Energy stuff?" said Max.

"Yes, but the problem was how to transfer the energy from us to them. The Zockrans were deteriorating fast and we knew if we didn't work it out very quickly, they'd all die."

"So what happened?"

"Late one night, DFEA engineers had a breakthrough. They discovered that Aura Energy could be transferred from humans to Zockrans via a device they built called a Re-Energizing Pod."

A small insert box appeared on the screen showing a metal cage with a domed top.

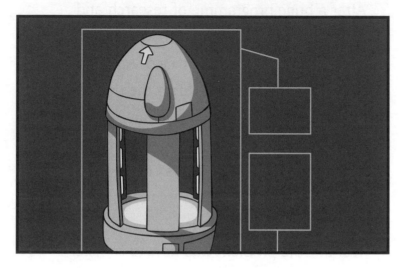

"If a human being enters one of these Pods," said Zavonne, "an Aura Energy transfer can take place, so long as Zockrans are within a hundred-metre radius. The more humans involved, the greater the amount of energy transferred. For the Zockrans to stay 'rejuvenated', these transfers have to take place frequently. DFEA engineers worked out that the Re-Energizing Pods need to be

de-activated before the 'Critical Point' is reached. For an average adult that point is reached after five minutes."

"Is that all?" asked Max.

"Yes," replied Zavonne. "Five minutes is sufficient. So long as the human spends no more than five minutes in a Pod at any one session, then this process can be carried out without causing even the slightest pain or danger to that human transferrer."

"Cool," whispered Max.

"Anyway," continued Zavonne, "when the crash-landed Zockrans were fully recovered, they told us they wished to return to Zockra. We agreed that a ten-person DFEA Unit would travel with them, along with ten of these Re-Energizing Pods. The members of this Unit would spend six months on Zockra using the Pods to transfer Aura Energy and thus make sure the Zockrans stayed in good health. When the Unit finished their six month tour, they would return to Earth and be replaced by another ten-person team for the next six months, and so on. That way, Zockran survival would be guaranteed."

"Wouldn't it be easier just to stop the Earth giving out so many pollutants?" asked Max.

Zavonne gave him a hard stare. "What do you think environmental campaigners spend their lives doing? Humans are constantly being warned of the effects of global warming, but they choose to ignore them."

"Point taken," nodded Max, "but did the Zockrans do anything for the DFEA in return?"

"They did," replied Zavonne. "The Zockrans promised they would act as an early warning system if any hostile alien race was ever planning an attack on Earth, and they made a commitment to defend our planet if war ever did break out."

"Is that why I'm here?" asked Max. "Are we about to be attacked?"

"We strongly suspect so," replied Zavonne. "We've just received a distress signal from the Zockrans. Last night, planet Zockra was invaded and the current DFEA Unit was kidnapped. This has had an immediate effect on the Zockrans' health. They're in a critical condition."

"So you're sending another DFEA Unit up there?"

"No, Max," replied Zavonne. "We're just sending you."

CHAPTER 4

"You're sending me alone?"

"That is correct."

"But why me? Why not an adult DFEA Operative?"

"One of the reasons I recruited you in the first place was because of your exceptional agility and contortionist skills," Zavonne explained. "I believe those unique qualities will be central to this mission and that's why I've selected you above an adult Operative. We don't know what we'll be dealing with up

there, and your special abilities may well give you the edge in a dangerous situation."

"OK," nodded Max, "but there are ten people in the DFEA Unit. The combined Aura Energy they can transfer will surely be much greater than the amount I can give."

"That's true," said Zavonne, "but you'll be able to provide enough energy to keep the Zockrans alive – until the kidnapped Unit are discovered and released."

"How long will my energy transfer last?"

"We have been looking into this," replied Zavonne. "An adult can stay in a Pod for no longer than five minutes. DFEA engineers have calculated that for a child this time period should be reduced to two minutes. You must leave the Pod when those two minutes are up. Failure to do so could result in a life-threatening situation. Do you understand?"

Max nodded seriously as Zavonne pressed straight on. "We can get you to Zockra incredibly quickly in one of our spaceships. The speed you'll be travelling at is so fast that no radar on earth will be able to pick it up. But before you set out, you'll need to complete a brief training module. You must go to the DFEA's hidden Space Base immediately – there is no time to lose."

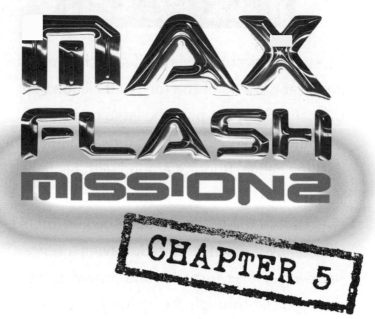

CHAPTER 5

Max's dad checked his rear-view mirror. There
was no other car in sight on the isolated
country road. They'd been driving for just
under an hour and had followed Zavonne's
instructions to the letter.

"Be careful," he said, with a worried
expression on his face. He gave his son an
affectionate squeeze on the shoulder. "We
want you brought back down to Earth as
quickly as possible."

Max gulped nervously, and got out of the car.

He stepped over to a very tall stretch of privet hedge at the side of the road and climbed up the bank. Stepping past the large patch of daffodils, he dipped his head forward, straight into the hedge. Rooting around with his right hand, he finally found the small metal dial and twisted it to the left as Zavonne had instructed.

Instantly the hedge parted, leaving a very narrow gap. Max turned round, waved at his dad, and slid through the opening. As soon as

he was past it, the hedge slid shut.

In front of him was a long path that cut through some trees. Max hurried forward until he saw a stone square on the ground in front of him. The stone began moving to reveal an opening. Max stepped forward and slid

down a chute into total blackness, crashing into a room a few moments later. He picked himself up, just as a series of spotlights came on illuminating a line of arrows leading off into the distance. Max followed the arrows until he reached a high, steel door.

What shall I do? Hang around until someone comes, or knock?

He'd just raised his left fist to knock, when a panel in the door opened and a man wearing a dark green jumpsuit and some sort of radio microphone appeared.

"Operative Hunter," the man said by way of introduction. "You must be Max."

Max nodded.

"We need to get straight down to work," said Hunter, ushering Max through the door and down a narrow, dimly-lit corridor. As Max struggled to keep up with Hunter, he heard strange noises all around him – twisting metal, grinding machines and whirring motors.

Finally Hunter stopped in front of a door on the left, swiped some sort of card and disappeared inside. Max followed and found himself in a whitewashed room as large as an aircraft hangar.

Around the walls were hundreds of pieces of silver equipment, all gleaming under bright lights. They came in all shapes and sizes, some no bigger than a football, others at least thirty metres high. Each piece was covered in buttons and levers.

"Unreal!" murmured Max.

"Right," said Hunter briskly, "the Zockrans are deteriorating rapidly so we need to get you up there fast, but as Zavonne explained, I need to give you a crash course in space survival."

Max listened anxiously.

"Firstly, we need to fit you with a spacesuit."

Hunter pressed a panel on the wall and a long metallic arm shot out, with a perfectly folded garment. Hunter lifted it off and passed

it over to Max.

"It goes over your clothes and MUST be worn at all times in space," said Hunter.

Max excitedly slipped on the spacesuit, wondering whether he could smuggle it home after the mission.

"The helmet's operated by that little green button on your chest."

Max pressed the button and a see-through helmet suddenly flipped out from somewhere on the back of the suit and over his head. Hunter motioned for him to put it back down so Max pressed the button again and the helmet snapped back into place.

"And now for your weightlessness training."

Hunter pointed to a glass door that faced into a large open space surrounded on all four sides and on its ceiling by mesh. Max grinned.

Of course! Floating in space – how cool!

He went through the door, which immediately closed behind him, and stepped on to the large blue mat that ran across the entire floor. Before he'd made it to the centre of the mat, he heard a loud whooshing sound and he was lifted upwards.

Instinctively he pawed at the air, trying to paddle himself back to the ground. But after a few seconds, he relaxed a bit and let himself get used to the feeling of zero gravity.

A minute later, Max was having the time of his life. He was flipping his body over, shimmying from side to side and hurling himself in every direction.

This is wicked! We have to get one for the school gym!

After five minutes, the whooshing sound began to fade and Max felt himself gradually falling back down onto the mat. He made it to the bottom and exited through the glass door, where Hunter was waiting for him.

"Now I need to give you a crucial bit of kit," said Hunter, retrieving a tiny white chip from one of his jumpsuit pockets. "This is a receiver/transmitter for your Speech Pulse Translator or SPT attachment. It'll ensure that you understand any creature you come across and that they can understand you in return. I'm just going to place it in your right ear. You won't feel anything."

The chip was painlessly in within seconds.

"Now I need ten minutes with you on the flight simulator."

They sat down together in an exact replica of a spaceship's cockpit. "Your craft has just been serviced," said Hunter, "and malfunctions – although they do happen – are very, very rare."

Well that's reassuring to hear! thought Max.

Hunter started explaining the huge array of buttons, switches and levers in front of him. Max's brain was soon reeling, but there was no let up. Just when he thought he had a grip on

the functions of the control panel, and had
been allowed to 'fly' the craft alone,
Hunter produced an interstellar map and
began to guide Max round the Hedra galaxy.

Finally, he paused.

"Have you got all of that?" he asked, looking concerned.

"Er ... kind of," Max replied.

"Good," said Hunter, "now it's time for your gadgets."

CHAPTER 6

Immediately Max's eyes lit up.

Gadgets! Bring them on!

Hunter reached into his jumpsuit. He produced three items and placed them on a white table to Max's left. Hunter picked up the first one, which looked exactly like a small roll of sticky tape.

"That is what we call a Direct Passage Pulveriser. Pull out a short length of this tape, stick it to the surface of a wall and hold the rest of the roll in your hand. Immediately, you and the section of wall you stuck the tape on to will be propelled forward at astonishing speed. Your momentum will smash through any type of obstacle and will keep going for fifteen seconds. It's quite a white-knuckle ride."

Max nodded and placed the tape in one of the pockets of his spacesuit.

"Next is a Zing-Board," said Hunter, handing Max a tiny silver skateboard, no bigger than the one Max had in his version of Monopoly.

"I don't think this will get me very far," Max said doubtfully.

"There's a tiny blue button on the underside of this Zing-Board," replied Hunter. "If you press that, the board extends to full size and will travel on any surface at the speed of light."

"Brilliant!" said Max, turning the board over in his hands. "Can I keep it when I'm back on Earth?"

"You know the rules, Max," Hunter said with a stern look, "each gadget can only be used once."

Max grimaced. His mates would go crazy over that board.

"And your third gadget is called a Net Can."

Hunter picked up an ordinary looking drinks can.

"Peel back the ring pull," he explained, "and whoever is standing directly in front of you will be instantly wrapped up and sealed in a tight net made of the highest quality, cut-resistant rope."

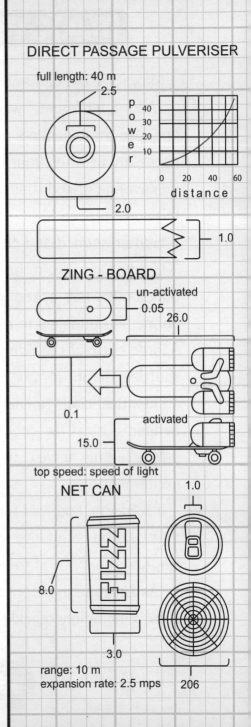

DIRECT PASSAGE PULVERISER

full length: 40 m

2.5

p
o
w
e
r

40
30
20
10

0   20   40   60

distance

2.0

1.0

ZING - BOARD

un-activated

0.05

26.0

0.1

activated

15.0

top speed: speed of light

NET CAN

1.0

FIZZ

8.0

3.0

range: 10 m
expansion rate: 2.5 mps

206

Max took the can and pocketed it carefully.

"And don't forget," warned Hunter, "you may only use these gadgets when absolutely necessary or when your life is in danger."

"Zavonne drilled that into me on my first mission," replied Max.

Hunter nodded and checked his watch. "OK," he said, "we're bang on schedule." He pulled out what looked like a very slim mobile phone and punched in a sequence of numbers. A large circle of the floor slid open and a space shuttle rose up from below. At the same time, an identical circle opened in the roof of the hangar.

Max felt his nerves jangle with tension and excitement.

If someone had told him a few months ago that he'd be going into space he'd have laughed them out of town.

"As Zavonne mentioned, we can get you to Zockra incredibly quickly in this craft. The

flight panel inside looks exactly the same as the simulator you tried out. Remember, you will be flying on autopilot, so just sit back and enjoy the ride."

"Right," said Max, swallowing nervously.

Hunter stuck out his right hand and they shook. "Good luck, Max," he said, "I'll see you on your return."

Max walked over to the flight of stairs that led up to the shuttle's cockpit. He climbed to the top and took a quick look round the hangar. Hunter was at a large console, rapidly flicking a whole series of flashing switches.

The door of the craft swung open and Max stepped inside. The cabin was circular and as Hunter had told him the flight panel was an exact replica of the simulator. Max sat down on the low black chair and two steel seatbelts eased out from the wall, dropped over his shoulders and clicked tightly into place.

MAX FLASH

Hundreds of yellow and blue dials flashed
on the flight panel in front of him and the
noise of rumbling engines suddenly flooded
the cabin a few seconds later.

Max felt his pulse racing.

*I cannot believe what is about to happen.
I'm going into space!*

He saw a digital display appear on the flight
panel with the number 5 and quickly flipped
on the helmet of his spacesuit. As the cabin
began to rock violently, Max closed his eyes
and began to count.

5, 4, 3, 2, 1, LIFT OFF!

The cabin suddenly shot upwards and Max's
stomach flipped. His whole body shook from
the sheer speed of the craft.

This is mad!

After a few minutes, the shuddering
disappeared and it suddenly felt like the
shuttle had stopped. Max realized that he
must be outside the Earth's atmosphere.

After half an hour had passed, the shuttle started slowing down and a hissing noise filled the air outside. The craft went slower and slower, until it finally juddered to a halt.

Have I arrived at Zockra already? thought Max, amazed. As the seat belts retracted and the door shot open, muggy air drifted inside the cabin.

Max took a very deep breath, stood up and flipped off the helmet of his spacesuit. Very hesitantly he walked through the cabin door.

He immediately regretted this move.

The most bizarre thing he'd ever seen was advancing towards him. Its long, thin body and oversized head were odd enough, but then Max's jaw dropped as he saw the four eyes and the mouth that resembled a semicircle of green jelly. It had ten extra-long fingers on each hand, and was wearing a tiny peaked cap on its head and a piped pink suit that was at least five sizes too small.

"Hey dude, don't freak out!" cried the creature, seeing the look of horror on Max's face. "I'm the welcoming party!"

CHAPTER 7

The welcoming party was an alien called Arcan who worked for the Inter-Planetary Rail Company. He drove a vehicle called a Planet Hopper, which looked a bit like a very hi-tech underground train, but with just two carriages, one for him and one for the passengers. He'd invited Max to sit up front with him and they were already speeding past dazzling planets, giant star formations and weird multicoloured moons. Max was glad that the Speech Pulse Translator was working, or both he and Arcan would be feeling very confused.

"The Zockrans sent me to pick you up," Arcan explained. "You touched down on a Hedra Docking Station. Your shuttle will be fine there – and now I'm taking you to Zockra."

Arcan's green jelly mouth suddenly turned up with pride. "I've had most types of creature in my Hopper, but never an Earthling. This is far out!"

"Yeah," nodded Max nervously, "this is DEFINITELY far out."

"The Zockrans are in a bad way, my friend," said Arcan, suddenly looking very serious. "I heard about the kidnap of that Earth crew. Bad news, dude, very bad news. The Zockrans are still alive, but they desperately need some of that Aura Energy. I guess you've come to fizz them up a bit?"

"That's right," nodded Max. "I'm going to do an energy transfer. But I need to get there fast."

"No problemo, kid!"

Arcan kicked the accelerator pedal and the Hopper scorched forward. Max noticed a thin black cord above his head and grabbed it to steady himself.

After a few minutes of high-speed flying, Arcan hit the brakes on the Hopper and hovered down towards a yellow planet that was covered with tiny lakes.

"This is Zockra, amigo," said Arcan, "and that building over there is the Command Centre."

The doors of the driver's carriage sprang open and Max held out his hand for a handshake. One of Arcan's long fingers shot forward and wrapped itself around Max's hand. Arcan then held out another finger. This one was holding a tiny strip of silver. "This is a Hopper Hurry Card," he explained. "Press this side and I'll come and pick you up from any place in the Hedra galaxy."

Max thanked him and tucked the silver strip

into one of his spacesuit pockets.

"Thanks for the ride, Arcan. Maybe see you around."

"I'm sure you will," grinned Arcan.

Max stepped out of the carriage and Arcan flicked the doors shut. The sticky yellow goo on the ground sucked at the soles of Max's boots.

The Hopper surged off and out of sight. Max studied the Command Centre for a few seconds and was about to head for the door when he heard a strange hissing sound behind him.

He flipped round and saw a silver and purple spaceship hurtling straight in his direction.

CHAPTER 8

Max looked round in panic. There was no time to run. As the craft thundered nearer, he suddenly spotted a tiny metal grille on the ground. The spaceship was nearly upon him and he acted immediately. Forcing his feet off the sticky yellow goo, he threw himself downwards, and just managed to squeeze himself through the narrow bars of the grille. The spaceship crashed forward, missing his head by millimetres.

Max held on tightly to the bars. He looked

down and was faced with nothing but blackness. The sound of the attacking spaceship faded into the distance, but he waited a good five minutes before he cautiously threaded himself back out through the bars.

Emerging, he saw with relief that the silver and purple craft was nowhere to be seen. He sprinted over to the door of the Zockran Command Centre, pushed it open and found himself in a long room containing chairs, desks, computer equipment and digital monitors.

Amongst this furniture there were about fifty pale, silvery creatures scattered all over the floor. They were cylindrical in shape, with no separation between their heads and the rest of their bodies. Each of them was issuing small moans and every time they did so, their bodies rose a few centimetres off the ground and then fell to the floor again.

Max couldn't help staring.

These guys have nearly reached their sell-by date.

One of the creatures was larger than the others. He beckoned Max over to him with a long red finger.

"Max Flash," he wheezed. "I am Nineth – Ruler of Zockra. You have arrived just in time to save us. Please climb inside one of the Pods. They're stationed in that room over there."

With great effort, Nineth lifted his finger and pointed to a green door at the far side of the room.

"We will then activate the Pod," said Nineth weakly. "The Aura Energy you transfer will give us the boost we so desperately need, long before the machine reaches the Critical Point. In this way, you will re-energise us and will suffer no harm yourself."

Max helped Nineth towards the door and they passed through it. In front of them was a row of Re-Energizing Pods, just like the one Zavonne had shown him. Each one was covered with dozens of tiny, flickering yellow lights.

"The DFEA has told me that it will not be safe for you to be in there any longer than a couple of minutes," said Nineth.

"Do you think that will be long enough to re-energize you all?" Max asked.

Nineth nodded. "We cannot risk your safety,

Max," he replied. "There is so much else for you to do."

Max opened the door of the first Pod and stepped inside. He watched as Nineth pressed a switch on the outside of the Pod.

Immediately, a low humming

sound started up and Max felt as if his whole body was being prodded by gentle fingers. It wasn't an unpleasant experience and it certainly didn't hurt. As soon as two minutes were up, Nineth de-activated the Pod and the humming and the strange sensation stopped.

Max saw that the Pod could only be opened from the outside and he waited for Nineth to let him out. Even with this short burst of Aura Energy, Nineth looked much better. Together, they returned to the main room of the Command Centre. Everywhere, Zockrans were very slowly getting to their feet. Their features were now far more clearly defined and the moaning had stopped, but they still looked very weak.

"Thank you," said Nineth, "we badly needed that Aura Energy."

"How long do you think it will last?" asked Max.

"It's hard to tell because we're used to ten

people re-energizing us simultaneously. You must hurry and find the DFEA Unit."

"I know," nodded Max. "Have you got any ideas who kidnapped them?"

Nineth was about to reply when he spotted something over Max's shoulder.

"I don't know exactly who they are, but that is definitely their spaceship!" he hissed.

Max spun round.

Out of a large window he could see the silver and purple craft that had nearly mown him down less than fifteen minutes ago. It was hovering in space about a hundred metres away.

"That's them!" said Nineth angrily. "They are our attackers. They have kidnapped the DFEA Unit!"

CHAPTER 9

Before Max could say anything, the silver and purple craft suddenly boosted its rocket cylinders and started flying away from Zockra.

"Where are your spaceships?" asked Max. "I have to go after them!"

"We haven't used spaceships for years," Nineth replied, shaking his head sadly. "Fuel is in very short supply on Zockra. We use the Hoppers or the Splook Tunnel to get around."

"The *what* tunnel?"

"The Splook Tunnel. It leads you on to the

Ballistic Highway. There's an Entry Port over there."

"Great," said Max, "How do you travel in this tunnel? Do you have some kind of special cars?"

"Some people do," nodded Nineth, "but we Zockrans prefer to walk."

"To WALK!" Max exclaimed.

"Yes. It may take you several light years to reach your destination, but the Service Stations have excellent and quite reasonably priced menus."

Max groaned, but then remembered the Zing-Board he had been given by Hunter.

Max yelled goodbye to Nineth and sprinted to the Entry Port. He quickly pressed the button on the underside of the Zing-Board. It exploded into a full-sized board and the engine roared into life. Max dropped it on to the floor and flames spat out of the exhaust.

Max took a deep breath and jumped on to

the board. It whirred ferociously, its wheels buzzed and the whole board went a deep fizzing scarlet colour. It then catapulted Max forward at the speed of light, straight on to the madness that was the Ballistic Highway.

CHAPTER 10

The wind whipped past Max's face as the Zing-Board zipped forward. He whooped with exhilaration – normal skateboarding was nothing compared to this! This wasn't just fast; this was supersonic! He wobbled dangerously as the board took a sharp corner, but just managed to keep his balance.

What a ride!

Max was travelling on one of several hundred illuminated tracks that twisted and curved in every direction.

Moving along these tracks were giant steel cubes with square wheels that gave off millions of sparks. There were small one-wheeled oval crafts that looked like old-fashioned bathtubs on wheels. There was what looked like a yellow school bus, except all of the aliens were travelling on the roof of the carriage and playing some sort of game using a crusty slug-thing as a ball.

As Max became used to the sensation of travelling at this ridiculously fast speed, he began to think about his destination, or in this case, his lack of destination. He realized that he didn't have a clue where he was going, or even if he was travelling in the same direction as the purple and silver spaceship.

I need to get a plan together. And quickly!

But in the next instant he was faced with another, much bigger problem. A massive orange beast with a very flat head and ten fiery red eyes came hurtling down the Splook

Tunnel in the wrong direction – heading straight for Max in what promised to be the collision of the millennium.

Max tried to twist his Zing-Board on to the path to his right but it wouldn't budge. He looked up and saw that the orange alien was almost upon him. It would smash him off the track!

Sparks were flying off the orange creature's body. As the wind screamed past Max's ears he closed his eyes and...

CHAPTER 11

...felt a light tap on his shoulder.

Very slowly he opened his eyes.

The orange alien had managed to veer off Max's track and was speeding off to the right. Travelling right beside him now was a creature with a large, fat, bright green body, a long, thin pink nose and three black eyes. Its circular feet were resting on what looked like a grey surfboard.

"Can I see your licence, please?" it asked.

"Er, what?"

"Your Splook Tunnel licence," it replied, wearily. "We've been catching a lot of unlicensed kids on the Ballistic Highway recently, so we're doing spot checks."

I haven't got time for this!

"My licence?" said Max desperately. "I haven't got it on me."

The inspector shot Max three very suspicious looks with its eyes. "Not another one!" it exclaimed.

"After I've finished my business," said Max, "I'll nip back and get it."

The creature shook his head firmly. "I'm sorry, but I'm going to have to take you in."

"No!" pleaded Max. "I'm on an urgent mission to help the Zockrans."

The inspector's expression suddenly softened. "The Zockrans?"

Max nodded.

"Well that's a different matter, what are you doing for them? I've heard that they're in

trouble – are you here to help?"

Max heaved a sigh of relief. Maybe this alien could help him?

"I'm following a silver and purple ship that attacked planet Zockra," Max explained, "but I don't quite know where it's heading."

"Well, you're in luck. I know exactly where it's going, I pulled it over to check the paperwork earlier today. It's heading for Feronda."

"Feronda?" repeated Max.

The inspector nodded. "I stopped you just in time," it said, "we're very near the turn-off."

A minute later, the inspector pointed to a circular Entry Point that was looming up on them. He waited until they were almost parallel with it and threw a small grey pellet down on to Max's Zing-Board. The pellet let off a shower of sparks, before suddenly forcing the board off the track and shooting it towards the Entry Point.

In a second, Max was through the Point and flying straight down a ramp on to a paved walkway. He leaned back on the Board and it stopped abruptly with a ferocious squealing sound.

As he jumped off, the Board spluttered for a few seconds and then completely disintegrated.

Shame – everyone at school would have been well impressed with that!

Max scanned his surroundings. The walkway was about fifty metres wide and stretched up a steep hill towards a huge ball of white light in the distance.

The light seemed to be coming out of a building up ahead.

Max was jostled by a group of rowdy green serpent-like creatures and after steadying himself he quickly checked the sky. There were lots of spacecraft up there but absolutely no sign of the silver and purple one.

Where is it, who is on it and what exactly am I going to do when I track them down? Time's running out! I HAVE to recover that DFEA Unit soon or the Zockrans won't survive!

Max turned to the closest creature, a female alien with an indigo body and a plump red head.

"Good evening," he politely greeted her, thankful again for the SPT device in his ear. "Can you tell me where this walkway leads to?"

She smiled warmly at Max and then slapped him in the face.

CHAPTER 12

Max jolted backwards.

"What was that for?" he shouted, rubbing his sore cheek.

She grinned toothily and whacked him again.

He hopped out of her way and held up his arms for protection.

"It's a traditional greeting when you meet an out-of-towner round here," she explained.

A second later, all sorts of aliens were steaming over to Max and slapping, whacking and flicking him.

"OK!" Max yelled. "You've all made this out-of-towner feel very welcome. Now will someone please tell me WHERE WE'RE ALL GOING?"

All of Max's slapping well-wishers suddenly stood back.

"To the Stadium of Power of course!" replied the female alien. "It's the Feronda Festival!"

The alien looked surprised that Max hadn't heard of it.

"The Feronda Festival is the biggest event of its kind," she said. "People travel from all over the galaxy to watch it. There are hundreds of shows – magic, illusion, music, drama, the lot. But most of us are going to see the Showcase Battles."

"Sounds like fun," replied Max, "but you haven't seen a silver and purple spaceship, have you? I know it's coming to Feronda, but I can't see it anywhere."

"Silver and purple?" she repeated.

Max nodded.

Her cheerful expression was suddenly replaced with a frown. "I have heard a strange rumour involving a spaceship matching that description," she declared.

"What is it?" asked Max intently.

She leaned in towards him and lowered her voice. "People are saying the craft belongs to an alien race, who have only just thawed out after being trapped in ice for many, many years."

"Why were they trapped and who trapped them?" asked Max.

"That's all I know," she replied.

Did the Zockrans trap these creatures in ice? Is that what the kidnap is all about – paying the Zockrans back by taking away their source of Aura Energy? And if it was the Zockrans, why didn't Nineth mention it? Surely he would know about such an incident?

Max was so busy puzzling over this new

information that at first he didn't notice that the crowd was slowing down. Suddenly he realized he'd reached the stadium, and was passing through a huge archway.

He looked up. He was standing at the bottom of a giant staircase that swooped upwards towards the sky. He turned round to thank the alien for her helpful information but she'd been swept somewhere else by the crowd.

Max felt himself carried forward to the very top of the stairs. As he reached the last step, he gasped as his eyes took in the most remarkable spectacle he'd ever seen.

CHAPTER 13

There was a gigantic sports stadium in front of him, with massive banks of spectators facing down towards the oval pitch. The stadium was lit up with dazzling floodlights. The crowd was filled with some of the weirdest aliens Max had seen yet.

There were spindly blue creatures, with three hideously bulging heads. There were square metallic beasts with tiny red heads on top of which rested twisting, gold antennae. There were squat green monsters with no heads and

five eyes in the middle of their chests.

I need to track down the silver and purple ship and I need more info on the aliens flying it. Who are they? And why have they kidnapped the DFEA Unit?

He felt a finger prod his arm. "Do you want me to show you to your seat?" asked a yellow spotted alien carrying official programmes and a tray of disgusting-looking snacks.

"Er, no thanks," Max replied, "I'm not planning on hanging around. But I am on the lookout for a silver and purple spaceship. I think its owners might have just recovered from being frozen in ice. Does that ring any bells?"

A scaly purple tongue suddenly protruded from the alien's mouth and it stood pondering the question for a few seconds.

"I haven't seen the ship," it eventually replied, "but I believe the race you talk of are called the Guzzlets and they have indeed just woken up from a lengthy ice sleep."

"Do you know who froze them?" asked Max.

"Of course," said the alien, "it was the Earthlings."

"Really?" gasped Max nervously as he felt his cheeks go a deep shade of red, "Earthlings, you say?"

"Yes," it answered, suddenly arching its head forward and studying Max's face very closely. "Why are you so interested in this matter?"

"Er, it's a school project," Max replied weakly. "I'm late handing it in."

The creature moved even closer to Max and suddenly a spark of recognition came over its face.

"Surely not..." it muttered, eyes widening.

Max was starting to feel anxious and was keen to get away from this alien, but it had gripped him.

"YOU'RE an Earthling, aren't you?" it asked in wonder. "I remember seeing a picture of your race many hundreds of years ago when I was just a young alien."

"You're making a mistake!" said Max. "Just let me go!"

As Max tried to free himself, the creature roared: "WE HAVE AN EARTHLING HERE! A GENUINE EARTHLING!"

Pandemonium exploded in the stadium. Aliens were on their feet, staring and pointing at Max, with open mouths (in some cases seven per creature) and shouting "EARTHLING!" at the tops of their voices.

Before Max could react, hundreds of hands and claws and feelers were pushing and pulling him downwards. He struggled to break free but it was no good: he was being dragged down the seemingly endless row of steps, towards the pitch.

CHAPTER 14

"NO!" shouted Max desperately, as he crashed downwards. "Let go of me! I'm on a special mission. I mean you no harm!"

But his words were lost beneath the rising hysteria of the crowd and a minute later he found himself being bundled over the advertising hoardings and on to the pitch. He stumbled a few paces backwards and looked wildly up at the towering stands above him. Thousands of alien eyes were gaping at him, thousands of alien voices were shrieking

"EARTHLING!" It was terrifying.

And then suddenly a giant shadow spread over the stadium. Max looked up. The silver and purple spaceship was now hovering right above the pitch.

"Your cries have alerted us to the fact that you have an Earthling down there," boomed a deep voice from the ship. "Can you confirm?"

"Confirmed," answered a machine somewhere in the stadium.

Max was rooted to the spot, staring up at the giant craft.

"Permission to land?" said the deep voice.

"Permission granted."

So this is when I finally get to meet these Guzzlets and start trying to get the DFEA Unit released. I can't believe Zavonne didn't warn me about them!

The ship began its descent and stopped when it was about a hundred metres above the pitch.

"WELCOME TO THE TWO HUNDRED AND TWENTY-SIX THOUSANDTH FERONDA FESTIVAL!" screeched a tinny tannoy voice. "AND WHAT AN UNEXPECTED, LAST-MINUTE TREAT WE HAVE IN STORE FOR YOU TONIGHT. FOR THIS YEAR'S FIRST SHOWCASE BATTLE I GIVE YOU TWO OF HISTORY'S MOST BITTER RIVALS. IN THE LEFT CORNER, WE HAVE A REAL HUMAN EARTHLING. IN THE RIGHT CORNER ARE TWO VICIOUS ICE MEN – THE GUZZLETS. LET'S GET READY TO RUUUUUUUUUUUUUMBLE!"

The crowd erupted with excitement.

Max swallowed anxiously and made a scary calculation.

Spaceship filled with human-hating Guzzlets + crowd roaring in excitement = extremely serious trouble.

Two holes appeared on the underside of the spaceship and two steel ladders shot out. A second later, two huge creatures emerged and

began climbing down on to the pitch. They had silver and purple striped bodies and powerful-looking arms. Their heads were triangular and each had three glaring eyes and mouths that were full of metal teeth that were snapping like shredders. In contrast to their vast bodies they each had two thin, flamingo-like legs, and Max noticed that their bodies were covered in a thick layer of ice. Sub-zero steam surrounded them and Max caught the chilly air on his face. He shivered.

These two look pretty dangerous!

"FIGHT! FIGHT! FIGHT!" chanted the crowd.

The massive Guzzlets took a few steps foward in Max's direction.

"Your people trapped us in ice for hundreds of years," boomed one of them. "Now it's time for our revenge!"

"Can't we just talk this over?" Max suggested desperately, slowly backing away from the menacing aliens.

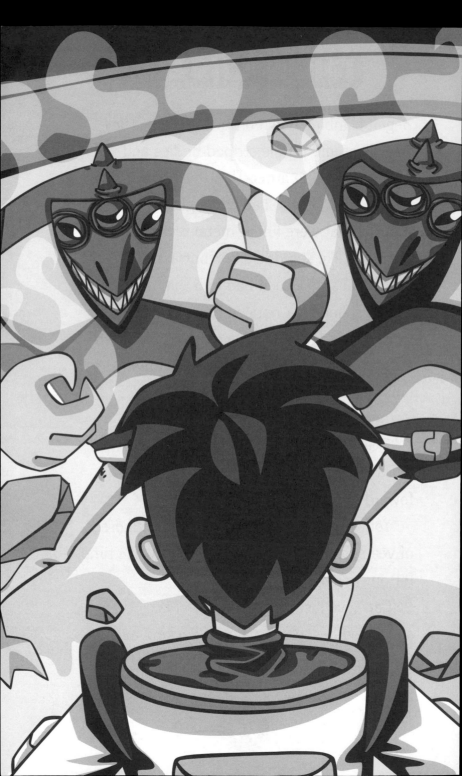

But a chat was the last thing on the Guzzlets' minds. Without any warning, a purple tentacle shot out from the first one's stomach and flung Max backwards. He crashed against one of the hoardings. Another tentacle lashed out, this one from the second Guzzlet. It curled itself round Max's head and he suddenly felt the blood being drained out of him. Using all of his strength, he wrenched the tentacle off him and thwacked it to the ground. The Guzzlet snorted furiously. There were boos and bellows from the crowd.

If I don't get out of here soon, I'll be mashed.

A third tentacle whipped out from the first one followed by a fourth from the second. These lashed against Max's chest, lifted him ten metres in the air and catapulted him backwards again. He thudded on to the pitch and struggled to his feet. The Guzzlets roared victoriously and came stamping towards Max.

He gulped, and desperately wished he still had the Zing-Board.

Wait! The Net Can!

Max swiftly pulled his second gadget out of his pocket, but to his horror, the ice coming off the Guzzlets had made his fingers so cold that they just couldn't activate the ring pull.

"NOOOOOOOOOOOOOOOOOOOOOOOOO!" yelled Max.

CHAPTER 15

One of the Guzzlets reached out and snatched the can, turned it towards Max and pulled the ring.

Immediately, a huge rope net shot out, encircled Max's body and tied itself very tightly around him. The crowd roared rapturously. The Guzzlets looked at each other with wide open mouths and both began to roar with laughter.

Max stood there feeling ridiculous. He'd been captured with one of his own gadgets. *That wasn't meant to happen!*

A few metres away, the Guzzlets were loving every moment. They waved at the crowds and started taking bows. As the roars got louder they puffed up their chests and threw their arms in the air, and set off on their lap of honour.

Max got to work. He knew this was his one chance – he only had seconds to get it right.

When the rope had shot over him, he'd managed to squeeze both of his hands into the space where the knot tied itself. This gave him a small circle of space to work in and he lost no time. Twisting and pushing out his wrists, his hands worked the gap and slowly the rope started to open. He took a quick glance at the vain Guzzlets. They were still bowing and waving.

The opening in the net was nearly big enough now. He gave it one further twist and then immediately compressed his body and started to push it out through the hole.

In ten seconds he was out.

The crowd started screaming in alarm and the two Guzzlets spun round.

"Sorry, boys, can't hang around!" shouted Max, as he ran off at full speed towards the other side of the pitch.

The Guzzlets immediately began to chase after him and as Max ran he felt a succession of tentacles shooting out at his back. He sidestepped some and whacked the others aside, but they were gaining on him. He lashed out in every direction, desperate to stop one of them wrapping itself around his body and squeezing him to death.

And then something terrible happened.

The Guzzlets sprung forward and flew over the top of Max. They came crashing down about twenty metres in front of him and turned to face him with hate-filled expressions.

Max made a snap decision.

There's only one way I'm going to get out of here alive.

Instead of running away from the Guzzlets he started to race straight towards them. As he

picked up speed, he suddenly dived to the ground and crashed forward on his knees across the earth. The Guzzlets leaned down to try and grab hold of him, but their bodies were too big to react quickly enough. Max skidded over the turf and careered right between one of the Guzzlets' legs and out through a door on the stadium wall.

Three tiny yellow aliens with oversized star-shaped heads jumped into the air in fright. Beyond them was some sort of space-park, with a solitary red ship parked up against a large white wall.

Max blocked out the howls of rage from the stadium and frantically sped towards the red ship. Its walkway was open and a pink-coloured alien with a long pointed head and six chunky arms was standing outside, flicking through a newspaper.

Max ran straight up the walkway.

"Hey!" shouted the alien, but Max barged

him aside and sped through a metal door at the far end of the walkway. He slammed the door shut behind him and heard the pink creature pounding the door.

Max bolted the door and turned round. He found himself on the ship's flight deck. It was empty. He sprinted over to the huge control desk and desperately checked out the hundreds of buttons and switches.

I have to free that DFEA team before the Guzzlets get to me. They must be planning a revenge attack on Earth and we need protection from the Zockrans!

A large black button on the desk declared 'ENGINE IGNITE'.

Sounds good.

Max was about to press it when he felt something cold and steely against his cheek. He looked round and found himself staring straight into the barrel of a giant silver gun.

CHAPTER 16

Holding the gun was a very tall and very thin alien. Its dark green skin was tight on its body as if it had been stretched to fit. It had two heads, each with one massive eye.

"Who are you that dares break into a Thargon Commander's ship?" demanded the angry creature.

"I'm SO sorry," smiled Max weakly, not sure which head he should be speaking to. "I didn't realize you were a Commander, I just thought you were an average Thargon."

Max heard shouts and the noise of stampeding feet outside the ship.

It's the Guzzlets plus whoever else wants to see me pummelled!

Max felt the sweat running down his forehead. Before the Thargon Commander could do anything, Max reached across and pressed the ENGINE IGNITE button. The roaring sound of engines exploded and the ship leaped upwards.

The Commander clicked off the safety catch on the gun.

"What's going on, sir?" shouted a voice at the back of the flight deck.

Two more Thargons were standing in a doorway, their weapons trained on Max.

One gun facing me isn't ideal, but three?

But then Max saw a circular yellow panel on the floor and realized what he had to do. As the three Thargons closed in on him, Max retreated, stepping back until he reached the circular panel on the floor of the deck. The Thargons didn't take their eyes off him and a second later they too had unknowingly stepped into the circle.

Max hurled himself into the air and somersaulted over the aliens' heads, kicking out and activating a wall button labelled EJECT.

A roof panel flipped open and the Thargons were shot straight out. A fierce blast of air tried to steer Max out too, but he clung tightly on to a steel bar and a couple of seconds later the roof panel closed.

Max let go of the bar, and dropped back down on to the deck.

Out of the viewing screen, he watched as the shocked and furious Thargons fell back down to Feronda.

Max jumped down on to a high-backed chair and took a closer look at the control desk. There were hundreds of buttons and levers on the desk, but only a few were marked with signs.

Luckily, Max recognized the symbol for throttle, and hit it. The Thargon spaceship started increasing its speed.

I urgently need to get to the Guzzlets' home planet. But how am I going to find it?

He pulled out the interstellar map and studied the Hedra galaxy. As he scanned the stars and moons he finally spotted a tiny planet faintly marked with the word 'Guzzle'.

Yes!

Max couldn't help smiling to himself.

I know where I'm heading now. Full speed ahead!

But a second later, the smile was swiftly erased from his face, as the Thargon spaceship took a direct hit from a thunderous missile.

CHAPTER 17

Max held up his arms to shield his face as his body thudded against a huge rack of equipment and he was thrown against the deck.

He staggered to his feet and ran back to the control desk.

Out of the viewing screen he saw the silver and purple Guzzlet ship. An orange flame exploded from its underside as another missile started powering its way towards the Thargon craft, intent on destruction.

Max lunged for the controls but he was too late. The missile smashed into the front of the Thargon ship and Max was knocked off his feet again.

I need to hit back!

Max stumbled back to the desk and frantically searched for a MISSILE LAUNCH sign, but he couldn't find one. And another flame had just burst into life on the Guzzlet ship and would soon be launched at him.

He looked around desperately and noticed a red lever on the far right-hand side of the control desk.

Give it a go! I've got nothing to lose!

As the Guzzlet missile screeched through the air, Max yanked the lever down to the left and miraculously the Thargon ship crashed to the left. The Guzzlet missile whistled past and exploded in a fireball somewhere behind the Thargon ship.

You missed that time, suckers!

But two more Guzzlet missiles had already been launched. Max grabbed the lever and steered the Thargon ship through the line between the incoming rockets. His directional skill was perfect as he just managed to miss both missiles.

I'm getting the hang of this! It's like playing a computer game.

Another Guzzlet rocket was launched and Max tilted his ship to the right, narrowly avoiding a hit. But then Max noticed a turquoise light flashing on the control desk, to signify that fuel was running low.

Now is NOT a good time to run out of fuel!

Max stared at the viewing screen. He could see the lit tips of a row of bombs at the rear of the Guzzlet ship.

I'll be a sitting target!

He scanned the space outside his viewing screen and noticed a series of very dense dust-clouds. There were at least twenty of them.

Max pulled the lever sharply to the right. The Thargon ship lurched towards the dust-clouds. A few seconds more and it had dipped behind the first one. He moved swiftly behind the second and third clouds and came to rest behind the fourth. It was a risky strategy but he didn't have another one.

He studied the viewing screen. The Guzzlet ship was now out of sight.

But it won't be long before they come hunting for me.

He nudged the lever and took the Thargon ship behind the fifth, sixth, seventh, then eighth cloud. He waited for a minute and nothing happened.

He nosed the front of the Thargon ship a tiny bit forward and then quickly pulled it back as he saw the Guzzlet craft loom into view.

Another minute went by and he snatched another look out of the viewing screen. The Guzzlets were starting to move off. They were going pretty slowly and cautiously but it was definitely in the opposite direction.

Max breathed a deep sigh of relief.

Safe ... at least for the moment.

He cruised out from behind the eighth dust-cloud and looked out at the orange tail lights of the Guzzlet Spaceship. He flicked the CABIN LIGHTS OFF button. Immediately the Thargon ship descended into darkness, the flight deck only illuminated by the thousands of tiny lights on its control desk and the shimmering stars outside. He touched the lever and the ship floated forward. He needed to keep the Guzzlets in his sights while making sure that they didn't see him.

He knew what he had to do. He had to follow the Guzzlets until they led him to planet Guzzle. Then he needed to find and release the DFEA Unit. But time was rapidly ebbing away and he was ever more wary of the fact that the Zockrans' survival completely

depended on him.

He was absolutely certain that 'failure' was not a word in Zavonne's vocabulary – he couldn't return to Earth until the DFEA Unit had been found, the Zockrans properly re-energized and his planet protected from possible attacks once more.

MAX FLASH MISSION2

CHAPTER 18

Max trailed the Guzzlet ship and as he did so he noticed a sudden drop in the air temperature. He shivered and checked the ship's temperature gauge. The needle was quickly moving into negative territory. And then up ahead he watched as the Guzzlet ship began to descend. It was dipping towards a planet that was completely covered in ice.

This must be planet Guzzle – at last!

The cold was now sweeping through the flight deck and biting at Max's face and hands

just as it had when he'd faced the Guzzlet warriors in the stadium at the Feronda Festival.

Max followed the Guzzlet ship from a safe distance. He watched it land and waited until all of those on board had exited and headed into the only building in sight – a tall structure near the landing pad.

What will it be like outside? Will my spacesuit give me enough protection to survive even a very short period out in that hostile climate?

Max began a slow, smooth descent. With every metre covered the temperature dropped further. He felt his spaceship crunch on to the ice below and then he turned the engine off.

He flicked the switch to unlock the door and heard a loud click. A hatch on the left-hand side of the flight deck opened. Max flipped on his space helmet and walked outside, not sure what to expect.

The chill hit him like a powerful punch.

It was freezing multiplied by a million. The cold felt like a thousand knife points on Max's body, and his teeth immediately began to chatter violently.

Wherever he looked, there was ice. No wonder the Guzzlets wanted revenge against Earth for forcing them to live in these conditions for so long. Max spotted a large building through the swirling mist and struggled towards it. He made a mental note to never, ever moan again when it was a bit cold on a school morning. Compared to this that would be a two week beach holiday in the Bahamas.

Even though he was wearing his helmet, his eyes were crusted with ice and his ears felt like they were about to snap off the sides of his head. Finally he reached the building's white front door. He reached out a hand and just about managed to grab the handle.

But no sooner had he done that than a

robotic voice called out, "Enter your password."

In shock Max spotted the small entry panel beside the door.

"Enter your password," repeated the voice. "If no password is entered after this third prompt, security will be called immediately."

Max began to panic. Summoning security was not very high on his wish list.

He badly needed inspiration.

But none came.

"Calling security in five seconds," announced the voice. "Five, four, three..."

CHAPTER 19

"Hang ... hang on a sec," spluttered Max, his teeth chattering violently.

"Two," said the voice.

"STOP!" shouted Max.

The voice suddenly went silent.

"Thanks," said Max.

"No one's ever interrupted my countdown before," huffed the voice sulkily.

"Sorry about that," answered Max, "but I don't have the password and I really need to get inside."

"No password, no entry," retorted the voice sharply.

Come on Max, think, think! Maybe flattery will work...?

"I really admire you," said Max, trying to stop his body shaking from the cold.

A pause. "Why is that?" asked the voice.

"Well, it must take a supremely intelligent life form to operate an entry system."

"You can tell I'm a supremely intelligent life form?" enquired the voice hopefully.

"It's obvious!" cried Max. "Your voice has intelligence all over its electronic vocal cords."

The voice let out a giggle. "No one has ever praised me before," it gushed. "It's wonderful to finally be appreciated."

"But I suppose," continued Max, "your powers don't stretch to knowing anything about what goes on inside this building?"

"Yes, they do!" protested the voice. "I know *everything!*"

"I bet you don't know the location of the DFEA Unit?"

"Of course I do!" replied the voice. "They're being kept in the strongroom on the outer southern wall of this complex."

"Wow," said Max, desperate to get out of the cold, "that is very impressive. But I need to go in now."

"Are you sure you don't want to know anything else?" The voice sounded a bit disappointed.

"Not for the moment, thanks," smiled Max, "but I'll spread the word about your amazing abilities."

"Would you?" said the voice, perking up. "That would be great."

And with that, the door clicked open and a very cold but very relieved Max Flash entered the building.

The warmth hit him immediately and he stood there for several minutes, thawing out

his hands and feet.

He was in a long, narrow white corridor and he began running down it, wincing. His feet felt like outsized blocks of ice, but each step he took, although painful, did restore some feeling to them. Max spotted a sliding door up ahead. He peered round it and saw a large square room bathed in silver and purple light.

Max grinned – standing against the right wall were ten humans wearing shiny orange suits with DFEA emblazoned across the front in silver letters.

I've made it!

The Unit comprised five men and five women. Each of them was smiling and waving at Max. He waved back and started striding across the room towards them.

"Hey guys!" He beamed.

But in that instant, the ten members of the DFEA Unit completely vanished.

CHAPTER 20

What's going on?

Max looked at the empty space where the Unit had been and shook his head. They'd been there. He'd seen them with his own eyes. They hadn't been cardboard cut-outs, they'd been real, 3-D, living and breathing humans. So where were they?

As he grappled with this mysterious twist, twenty panels on the walls of the room suddenly slid open. A Guzzlet marched through each one.

"Welcome to planet Guzzle!" the largest and ugliest declared with menace. "A freezing, perilous dungeon!"

It's always great to hear someone talking up their home planet!

"I don't plan on taking a holiday here," replied Max, "shall we just cut to the chase? I've come to release the DFEA Unit."

"I'm surprised one so clever as you fell for our fake projections of your cronies," hissed the Guzzlet Chief. "You can work wonders with a Multi-Cryptonic Slide Projector."

"How very clever of you. Now if you don't mind I'll just get the Unit and we'll leave you and your Slide Projector alone together."

"Oh dear!" the Chief sighed dramatically. "You are so out of your depth here it's frightening. I almost feel sorry for you."

"The only thing that's frightening is your breath!" exclaimed Max. "I can smell it from here. Have you been drinking from a sewage pipe?"

The Guzzlet Chief spat out a huge blob of grey and mauve liquid that hissed and fizzed on the floor before burning itself out.

"You can mock all you like," sneered the Chief, "but nothing will stop us from gaining our revenge on your people. You meddling Earthlings stopped our plans for total intergalactic domination by freezing us – but our time has now come. With the Zockrans out of action, we can attack your pathetic little planet and make you all Guzzlet slaves. It's about time us Guzzlets took a nice, long holiday. And your planet, with all those beaches, cities and mountains, looks PERFECT!" He laughed at the look of horror on Max's face, and clicked his fingers.

Max looked up and saw the outline of some sort of contraption being lowered towards him on a thin metal pulley. As it got nearer he recognized it.

It was a Re-Energizing Pod.

The Guzzlet Chief shot Max a gruesome smile. "In just over two minutes' time you won't have the energy to save the day! Your rescue mission will be over!"

Max's brain whirred – the Guzzlets must have stolen one of the pods along with the DFEA crew – and now he was about to have all his Aura Energy drained out of him. He had to do something – and fast!

CHAPTER 21

Instead of trying to run away from the Pod, Max calmly walked up to the door and let himself in.

"A willing victim?" noted the Chief with a puzzled frown.

But Max had just hatched a plan.

It would require several elements to work at the same time, but it *was* possible.

"Strange – but no matter!" cried the Guzzlet Chief, throwing his hands up in the air. "IT'S SHOW TIME!"

The Chief walked over and hit the 'Activate' switch on the outside of the Pod. Max immediately felt the sensations he'd experienced when he'd re-energized the Zockrans back on Zockra. As the Guzzlets clapped their hands and roared approval, Max reached inside one of the pockets of his spacesuit.

Max knew he had a short space of time to make this plan work. He knew he had to leave the Pod immediately after two minutes were up. Max definitely didn't want to be inside this thing when the Critical Point was reached.

He brought out the Direct Passage Pulveriser, and pulled out a short length of tape.

Holding the roll in one hand, he reached out and stuck the tape to the front of the Pod. There was a huge spark of electricity, and the Pod crashed forward at blistering speed, smashing through the wall in front of it.

"STOP HIM!" shrieked the Chief as great chunks of rubble flew through the air. The

noise was deafening. But the Pod had only just started its journey. It sped through another room and clattered through the wall at its far side. Max pushed his arms against the wall of the Pod to steady himself.

But his relief at this blistering escape was suddenly overtaken by a weird sensation that was suddenly spreading over his body. It was as if hundreds of little sharp forks were pricking him.

I must be nearing the Critical Point!

Still the Pod continued on its frenzied path, bashing through a third, a fourth and a fifth room, leaving a devastating trail of bricks, stone and dust in its wake. Max stole a backwards glance. Through the great haze left by the Pod, Max could see the Guzzlet Chief and his orderlies running behind him.

The stabbing was getting sharper now and Max's brain was beginning to feel pinched and tight.

I have to get out of here soon!

The Pod sped on, leaving a vast hole in every wall it ripped through.

Max felt his brain going all fuzzy as if concrete was being tipped inside his head. His eyelids became incredibly heavy and he sensed he was losing consciousness.

Must stay awake. Must. Get. Out...

As the Pod flew through the seventh room, Max's heavy eyes spied a group of people huddled together in a corner. The Pod smashed through the far wall of the seventh room. This led to the outside and into the frozen wasteland beyond. The Pod thudded a few metres over the ice and snow and abruptly stopped.

The ten figures leaped to their feet and ran towards him. The first of the figures to jump through the smashed wall – a woman with short brown hair – hit the de-activation switch on the outside of the Pod and yanked open the door.

Max staggered a couple of steps forward and fell out of the Pod.

The woman caught him. "Operative Sandy Larsson," she said, "I head up this DFEA Unit."

Max felt as if a heavy, stifling blanket was being pulled from his body and brain. The prodding fork points seemed to vanish in the air. And he was so delighted to see Larsson and the others that he hardly noticed the freezing conditions this time.

"Great to meet you," replied Max, stretching his arms out in front of him and shaking his head to remove the last of the strange sensations. "There's a Thargon spaceship at the launch pad. You must fly back to Zockra. The Zockrans desperately need your Aura Energy. The ship is low on fuel so take some from the Guzzlets' craft before you go."

"You're coming with us," Operative Larsson said.

"I have some unfinished business here," he replied, jerking his thumb back in the direction of the Guzzlets who were streaming through the fifth room and nearly upon them.

"We can't leave you," protested Larsson.

"YOU HAVE TO!" shouted Max. "I KNOW WHAT I'M DOING!"

Larsson and the other DFEA members exchanged quick, uncertain looks.

"You're sure?" asked Larsson.

"Completely sure," replied Max. "PLEASE, GO NOW!"

Larsson nodded gravely and started running round the side of the building with her team right behind her, braving the swirling, icy mists and freezing temperature.

Max looked back at the fast approaching Guzzlets, reached into his pocket and hauled out the Hopper Hurry Card. Time to take a little trip...

CHAPTER 22

"You called, amigo?"

Max turned round and saw the very welcome sight of Arcan in his Planet Hopper. Max grinned and yelled, "Hey, Arcan! That was quick. Can you open the carriage doors?"

Arcan pressed a button and the two doors slid open.

The Guzzlets were now only a few metres away.

"In here, guys!" shouted Max. He ran through the first door into the carriage. The

Guzzlet Chief and his followers roared in anger and piled straight into the carriage. Max sped down past the seats towards the carriage's other door, looking back to make sure every Guzzlet was on board. When he was satisfied they were all in, he shouted to Arcan.

"CLOSE THE DOORS!"

Max knew his timing had to be perfect.

The second door started to close and Max made his move. He threw himself forward and just managed to slide through the gap before the door crashed shut.

Max had made it into Arcan's front carriage. He turned round and stared into the carriage behind.

The Guzzlets were completely freaking out. They were dribbling and shrieking and banging on the carriage doors.

Max pulled out his interstellar map, studied it for a couple of seconds and then told Arcan where to go.

"No problemo!" laughed the alien, slamming his foot down. The Planet Hopper soared away from the freezing planet Guzzle and arced upwards towards a bank of glittering stars.

"What have you been up to?" asked Arcan. "It looks like things have been getting seriously heavy."

"They have," nodded Max, "but it's nothing I can't handle."

As they sped through the sky, the sound of the Hopper's engine competed with the screams of the Guzzlets in the carriage behind them.

"May I?" asked Max after a few minutes, indicating the driver's microphone.

"Go for it," beamed Arcan.

Max turned the microphone on and cleared his throat.

"Lovely to have you Guzzlets on board," Max said into the microphone. "We'll be travelling at six thousand million light years per second and will be arriving at our destination shortly. Look out for the yellow-tinged nebula to your left, because you won't be seeing it again for quite some time."

Max could hear the moans and screeches of the locked-in Guzzlets.

"And don't forget to put any litter in the bins provided," added Max. "We don't want anyone messing up this marvellous transport system."

"You're a natural," laughed Arcan. "There are some Hopper driver's jobs going at the minute. Why not apply?"

Max grinned. "Maybe one day," he replied.

Arcan breaked suddenly.

"I believe this is your selected destination," he announced to Max.

MAX FLASH MISSION2

CHAPTER 23

The Hopper screeched to a halt.

Max looked at the station sign just outside the driver's carriage.

DELTA BLACK HOLE 1713.

Arcan shrugged his shoulders. "What do you want to do with that lot back there?" he enquired.

Max spied a button labelled TILT in front of him.

He pressed DOORS OPEN and followed this with TILT.

The Hopper's two passenger doors slid open and the train leaned steeply to the right.

The Guzzlets tumbled out of the carriage, straight into the mouth of the black hole.

"NOOOOOOOOOOOOOOOOOOO!" shrieked the Guzzlets, but it was too late. They were already being sucked down into the depths of the swirling mass.

Max and Arcan did a high five and then they both burst out laughing.

"You really showed those dudes," chuckled Arcan.

"I couldn't have done it without you," Max grinned.

"Where to next?" enquired Arcan.

"Back to planet Zockra!" shouted Max with relief.

Arcan flipped the Planet Hopper round and within minutes they were back on Zockra. Max clambered out of the Hopper and turned to say goodbye to Arcan. "Thanks for everything," he said.

"It's my pleasure," the friendly alien replied.

"If you're ever on Earth, I'll take you on a bus. It'll be a lot less cool than travelling in your Hopper though!" said Max.

And with that, Arcan waved and zoomed off. Max waited until the silver tail lights of the Hopper had disappeared over one of the six

horizons in view and then started walking over
to the Community Centre.

On entering, he stopped in his tracks,
amazed at the transformation of the place. The
Zockrans were buzzing round the place, no
longer pale, frail and desperately ill.

I did it! thought Max. *I saved them!*

Nineth picked his way through the crowds
and reached Max's side.

"Welcome back," he smiled, his face looking
far more alive than before. "Your colleagues
from the DFEA are currently sleeping after their
experiences. They were hoping to be up to bid
you farewell, but Zavonne is keen for you to
return immediately. I've arranged for your
spaceship to be brought here from the Hedra
Docking Station." Nineth placed his hands on
Max's shoulders. "Your bravery will never be
forgotten on Zockra," he declared.

"Glad to be of service," Max said proudly.

CHAPTER 24

Once he was back in the spaceship and heading for home, Max went over everything that had happened on his mission to the Hedra galaxy.

No one at school would believe even the tiniest fraction of it!

It had been a crazy trip and Max suddenly started to feel very sleepy. His eyes began to close. He would have slept the whole journey back to Earth if it hadn't been for the loud automated voice suddenly booming out from the flight panel.

"THROTTLE OVERRIDE! SHUTTLE TRAVELLING AT UNACCEPTABLE SPEED! ACTIVATE BRAKES."

Max opened his eyes and scanned the flight panel for a BRAKES control. It was nowhere to be seen.

"ACTIVATE BRAKES!" the voice repeated.

Max looked to his right at the ship's navigation screen which showed their exact position. They were nearly upon Earth.

Max looked at the flight panel again.

Where are the brakes?

He gulped in horror.

If I don't stop this thing soon I'll be dust.

Frantically, Max thought back to his session in the flight simulator with Hunter. He was sure Hunter had talked about the brakes but he had no recollection of where they were.

He checked the navigation screen again. The shuttle was rapidly descending and Earth was getting bigger and bigger on the screen.

"IMPACT IMMINENT!" announced the panel. "APPLY BRAKES IMMEDIATELY!"

Max threw himself against the flight panel, pressing every single switch he could reach in a desperate attempt to stop the craft.

The brakes must be somewhere!

And then he saw it. A small foot pedal wedged quite a way in beneath the bottom of the panel, with a narrow sign reading BRAKES.

What a ridiculous place to put it!

Max kicked his leg forward but he couldn't reach the pedal. He kicked out again, but still without luck.

"DANGER OF DEATH! DANGER OF DEATH!" boomed the panel voice.

Max looked at the navigation screen. He could see the DFEA Space Base rapidly approaching.

In a last, desperate attempt to avoid death, Max pulled his leg back and threw himself on to his front. He squashed his body down

against the floor and wriggled forward under the flight panel. He managed to get further than his leg had stretched but even this wasn't far enough.

"CRASH SITUATION! CRASH SITUATION!" bellowed the panel.

Straining every muscle, Max made one last attempt to activate the brakes, and just managed to catch the edge of the panel with his hand.

The spaceship came to a violent halt, causing Max to bang his head on the underside of the panel. He winced in pain and then slowly pulled himself out. He stared in horror at the navigation screen. The craft was hanging no more than fifty metres above the opening hatch on top of the Space Base.

If he'd been a fraction of a second later, he wouldn't have made it.

CHAPTER 25

Max guided the space craft into the docking station and breathed a huge sigh of relief.

Hunter was waiting at the bottom of the stairs with a very concerned expression on his face.

"I can't believe there was a throttle override," said Hunter when Max reached the bottom of the steps.

"I can't believe the brakes were so hard to get to!" replied Max.

Hunter frowned. "That must have been Operative Dawson. He's got very long legs.

He must have moved the pedal to suit his frame."

"Er, why didn't you check that out before you sent me up there?"

Hunter scratched his ear and looked embarrassed. "Time was tight, I couldn't cover every base. Looks like you did OK up there though! Once you've changed out of the spacesuit I'll take you to where your father is waiting. We contacted him when news of your return came through on the monitor, and he's anxious to see you."

Max pulled off the spacesuit with some regret – it was much cooler than his school unifom, that was for sure!

Hunter then led Max back to the hedge, which parted to reveal Max's dad's car parked by the side of the road.

"Well done, Max," said Hunter, and shook his hand.

His dad jumped out of the driver's seat and

gave him a hug. "I want to know everything. First of all, are you OK?"

"I'm fine, Dad. It's great to be back in one piece!"

As his dad steered the car back down the road, Max began a blow-by-blow account of his second DFEA Operation. By the end of the hour-long journey Max had told his dad pretty much everything.

His mum was waiting for them by the front door, when they pulled up outside the house. "Well done!" she beamed. "Zavonne wants to see you straight away."

She doesn't waste a second!

Max nodded and headed down to the cellar. Back in the Communications Centre, Zavonne's face was already on the plasma screen.

"You certainly cut it a bit fine to save the Zockrans," she observed coldly.

"I did it as fast as I could," Max replied defiantly.

Zavonne pursed her lips. "Operative Larsson has filled me in on your escapade on Guzzle. So those Guzzlets were planning on invading Earth and enslaving us all?" she asked.

Max nodded. "You might have warned me about them! Anyway, I think I've put the Guzzlets out of action for a while," he smiled.

Zavonne's expression remained frosty. "Let's hope so. And your gadgets – I trust you only used them in extremely dangerous situations?"

"Of course," Max replied.

"Then this debrief signals the successful end of your mission," noted Zavonne.

"Will there be another mission for me?"

Zavonne fixed him with her icy stare. "That remains to be seen."

Before Max could say anything else, the image of Zavonne fizzled out and the plasma screen turned blank.

Typical, thought Max. *Zavonne the ice queen would be right at home on planet Guzzle...*

EPILOGUE

In Black Hole 1713, as the Guzzlets were turning and spinning in the infinite blackness, one of their number hesitantly propelled himself over to the Guzzlet Chief.

"I suppose we should look on the bright side," suggested the junior Guzzlet. "I mean, we were encased in ice for hundreds of years. We're used to being stuck in places with a rubbish view."

The howls of the other Guzzlets could be heard in every galaxy within a one hundred million mile radius.

IT'S SOON TIME
FOR MAX'S THIRD TOP
SECRET MISSION...

MAX, AN ISLAND IN THE PACIFIC OCEAN HAS BEEN FLOODED BY A FREAK SURGE OF WATER. WE SUSPECT SINISTER FORCES AT WORK AND WANT YOU TO INVESTIGATE.

AN UNDERWATER ADVENTURE? I'LL DIVE STRAIGHT IN!

MAX WONDERED WHAT FEARSOME CREATURES OF THE DEEP HE WOULD BE FACING...

COLLECT THEM ALL!